ORBIT'S MONSTER NEBULA

Billy Baldwin
Liesl Bell

Decozen Books   New York   info@billybaldwinstories.com

Summary: Explore Orbit's monster-making laboratory and travel with her to Earth as she uncovers a plot to rid the universe of all monsters and close her Monster Nebula forever.

Library of Congress Number: 2021918491
ISBN: 978-0-9791882-5-1

Decozen Books
P.O. Box 3238
Sag Harbor NY 11963

billybaldwinstories.com
info@billybaldwinstories.com

Printed in Bulgaria

In a distant galaxy, hidden from sight, lurks the planet Gorgon.

Space travelers fear this planet, and for good reason!

It makes **monsters!**

I know what you're thinking. Monsters? No way! But it's true.

Hundreds of years ago, my great-grandfather, Professor Astroblast, realized that people love the dark, shadowy, unknown regions of their imaginations. So, he came up with a plan to replace the imaginary with something that would really scare them!

It worked! And our family has been making monsters ever since.

This is our Great Hall of Monsters, where legends have been created. We have monsters that protect treasures, challenge heroes, star in films, and occasionally devour evil wizards.

My name's Orbit, by the way.
That's me with the monstrous hair.
I'm the youngest scientist in the
Astroblast family.

These days, I run the family
business with the help of my best
friend, Bazoo. He's a Cyberbot, of course.

It gets lonely at times, without any other children to play with. But all these monsters running around makes for a dangerous playground. Luckily, I have my work to keep me busy.

When coming up with a new monster, my favorite design tool is my Holographic Illustration Simulator.

This is where the magic starts—
uploading the monster's design into
the Cellular DNA Milkshake Computer.
I begin mixing the monster's features.
I can add things like horns, feathers,
hair, wings, or flippers. I get to decide
if it crawls or flies, breathes fire, or
can crush a building with its foot. I
can even choose its eye color. When
I'm done, the machine creates a new
monster egg.

"Center the egg's trajectory, Bazoo. Activating the Nebula Chamber birthing sequence, now."

The Nebula Chamber stimulates an egg with solar light, giving it life energy. Then it bathes the egg in hydrogen, helium, and oxygen before hitting it with an electromagnetic pulse that shocks it to life.

"Grandpa, NO! STOP! That's the disintegration abort button!"

Whew, that was close! Grandpa is a super genius, really. But he's a little spacey these days. He loves to visit me and tinker about his old lab, but I've got to keep an eye on him.

"Transferring the egg into Accelerator Growth Chamber Four," Bazoo confirms. "Feeding tubes and atmospheric temperature set."

Pretty cool, huh? This is where the eggs will grow into monsters. "Come on, little guy, watch out for the wet floor."

Isn't this Burpa cute? I love when they take their first steps.

Of course, growing monsters isn't all we do here. All of our monsters go through rigorous training, learning how to scare, fly, breathe fire . . . you know, how to be monstrous.

"That's our fastest: Orgodrag!" I tell King and Queen Obi. "Sure to terrify even the best star pilots."

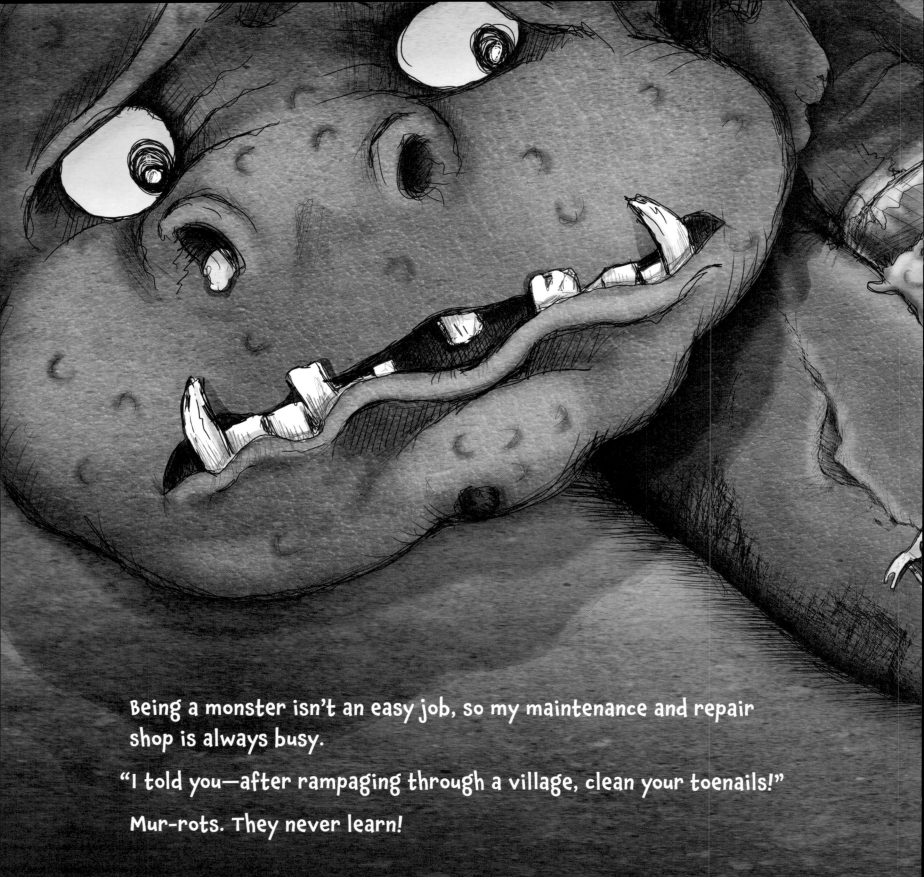

Being a monster isn't an easy job, so my maintenance and repair shop is always busy.

"I told you—after rampaging through a village, clean your toenails!"

Mur-rots. They never learn!

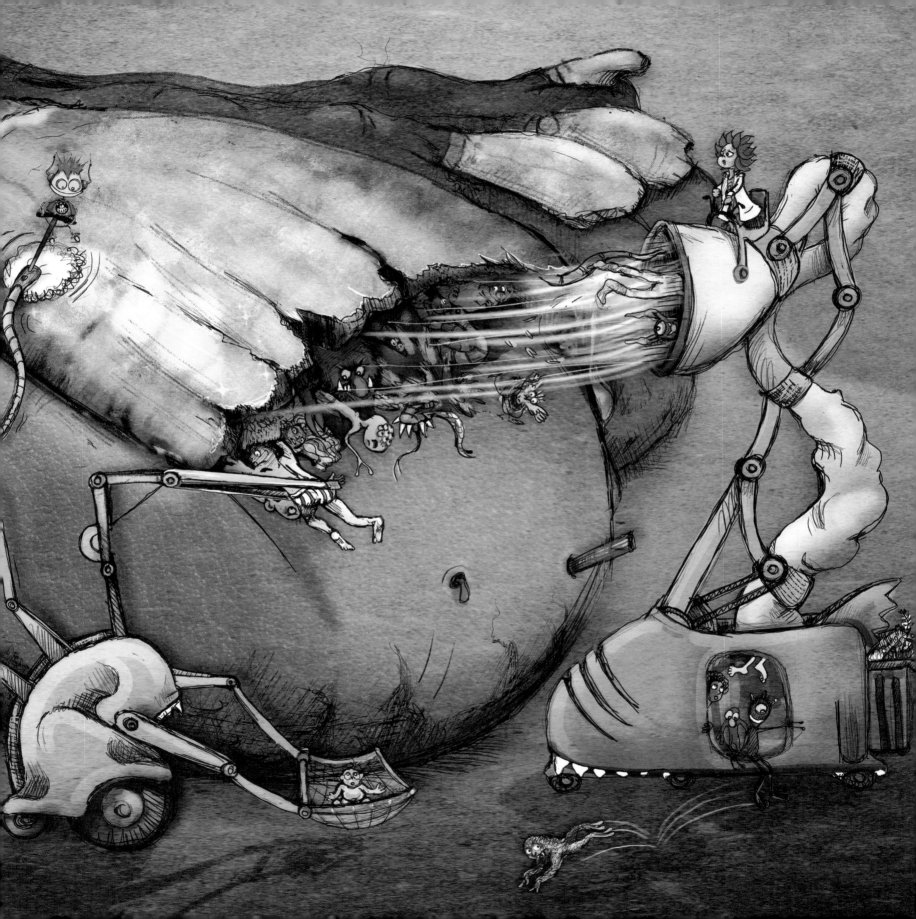

All of a sudden...

The galaxy monster tracker! It's sending out a warning signal.

"Orbit!" Bazoo shouts. "A monster is leaving its designated work zone."

Someone is taking my monster!

On the Planet Zebu...

"Inspector, a monster has taken Prince Obi. We found claw marks and monster hair on his scooter," an officer reports. "So far, no sign of the prince or the monster, though."

The chief alerts Head of the Intergalactic Council of Planets, Counselor Gurloff, and tells him what has happened to the prince.

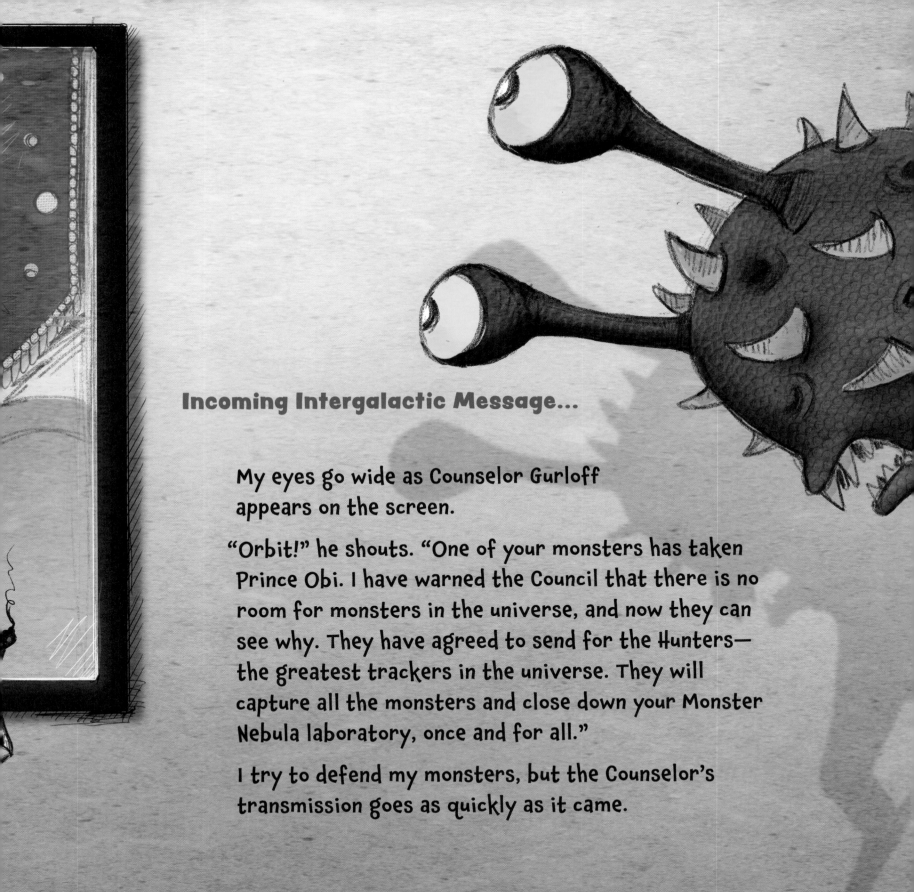

Incoming Intergalactic Message...

My eyes go wide as Counselor Gurloff appears on the screen.

"Orbit!" he shouts. "One of your monsters has taken Prince Obi. I have warned the Council that there is no room for monsters in the universe, and now they can see why. They have agreed to send for the Hunters—the greatest trackers in the universe. They will capture all the monsters and close down your Monster Nebula laboratory, once and for all."

I try to defend my monsters, but the Counselor's transmission goes as quickly as it came.

"Bazoo, we need to hide all monsters before the Hunters catch them. Direct the monsters into the Space Pod Minimizer. I've calculated their travel coordinates and entered them into the Monster Launcher. Load the pods. Fire One!"

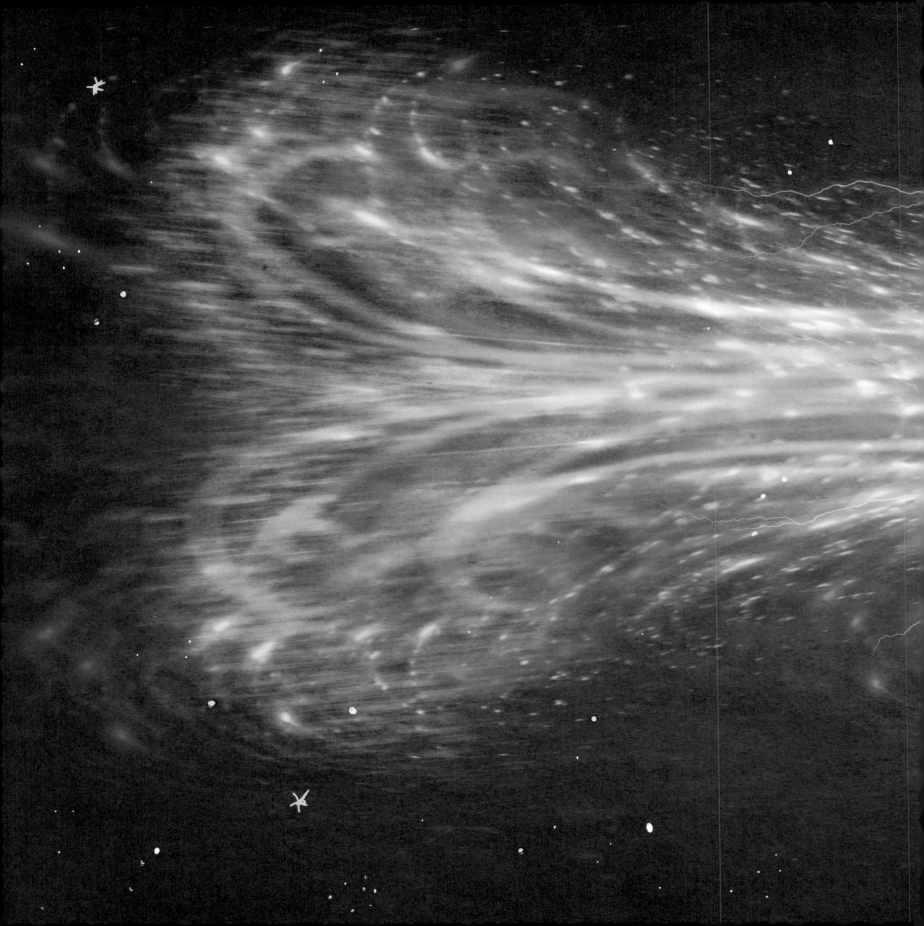

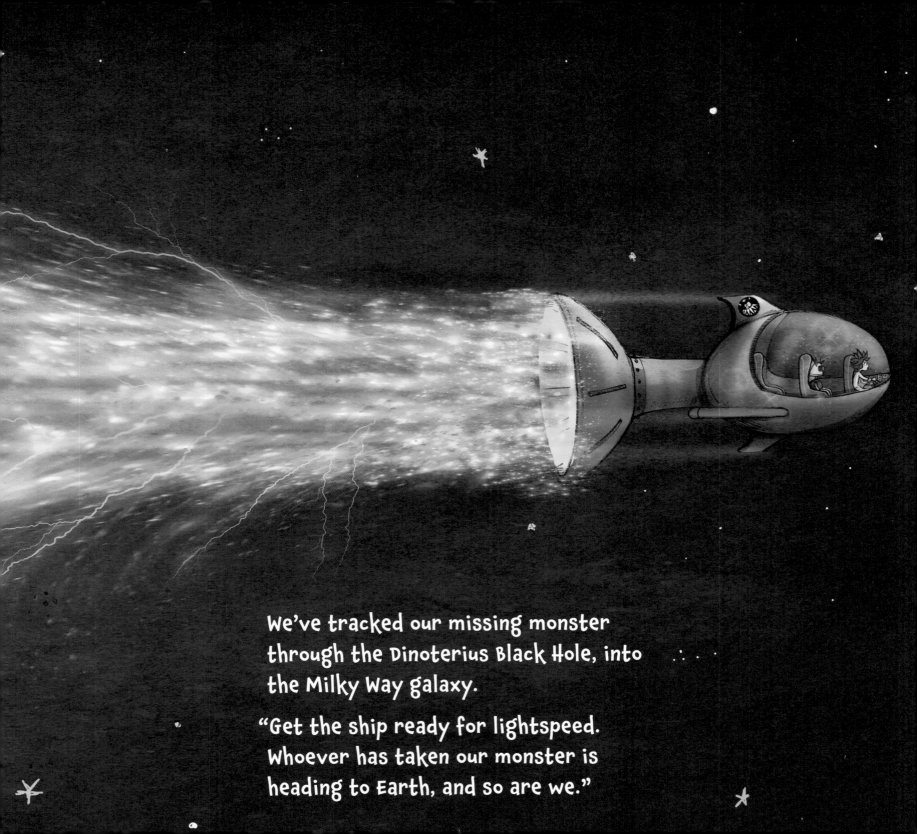

We've tracked our missing monster
through the Dinoterius Black Hole, into
the Milky Way galaxy.

"Get the ship ready for lightspeed.
Whoever has taken our monster is
heading to Earth, and so are we."

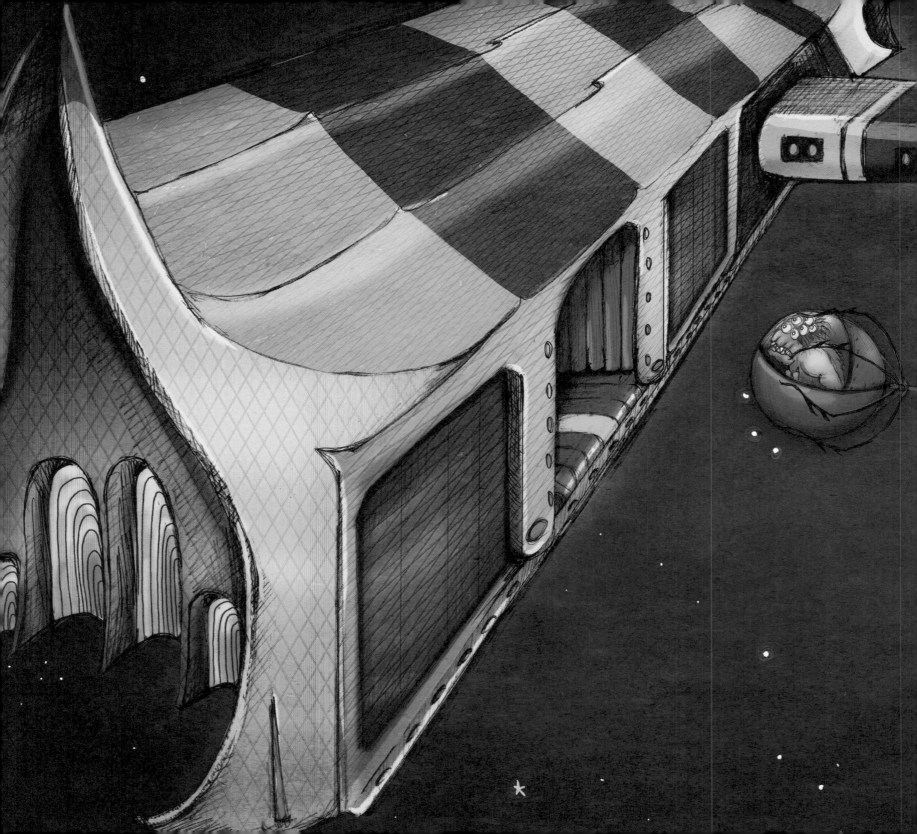

Meanwhile on the Hunters' ship . . .

"Captain, the last two monsters from Orbit's
Monster Nebula have been captured," the
first mate announces. "Should we—"

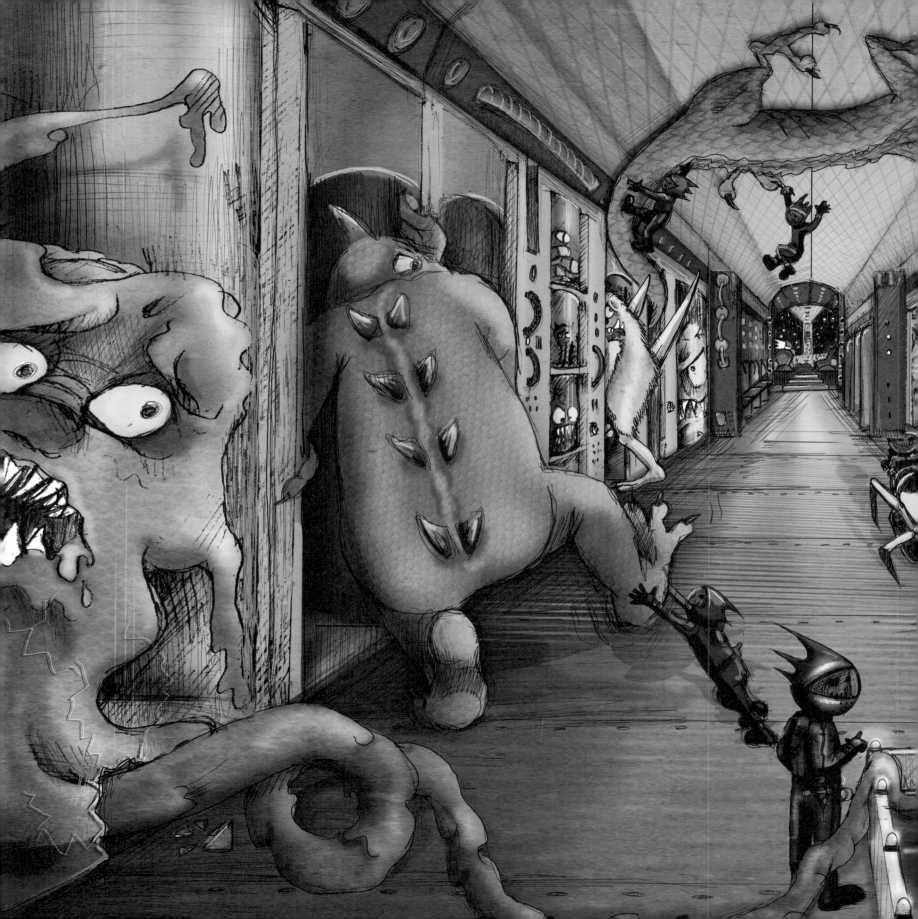

"No. Young Orbit has fled to Earth. She will lead us straight to Prince Obi and double our bounty. Now, stop playing with those monsters and secure them in their cells."

In an Earth prison deep underground . . .

"Bazoo, why is our monster imprisoned with the kidnapped Prince? Who did this? Something evil is afoot."

Uh-oh. The Hunters have found us.

I can't lose them, but maybe we can find a place to hide in that large city just ahead!

"There!" the prince shouts. "We can hide in that parade of humans celebrating some sort of Earth holiday."

But the Hunters aren't fooled!

"They've got us cornered!" I yell.

"Oh, no. This can't be good."

A ship touches down right in front of us.
Counselor Gurloff runs off the ship, grabbing
the prince. But the Hunters have realized his plan.
They cut off his path back to his ship.

The Counselor escapes with the prince, knocking me to the ground. "Your monsters terrified me and my family as a child, now it's my turn for revenge," he yells.

I jump to my feet, racing down the adjacent street to cut him off at the next intersection.

Bang!

"Nice shot, Orbit."

I capture the Counselor using a Monster Net Blaster. The Hunters place him under arrest.

The prince thanks me . . . with a kiss. Yeah, pretty sure
I'm redder than a boggleberry.

"What should we do with all these monsters on our ship?" the Captain asks.

"Captain, look around. These humans have a holiday—Halloween—that celebrates being scared. Let's release some of the monsters right here on Earth so they'll *really* have something to be scared about.

We deliver the first one to the
Himalayan mountains.

Another plays with natives
on a tropical island.

One is just in time for dinner in Japan.

And this little guy finds a home in a Scottish lake.

Everybody needs a good scare!